The Bicycle

Paavannan

Adapted from the Katha Award-winning story, "The Journey"

Translated from the Tamil by N Kalyan Raman

Art by Ayush Rajvanshi

& Mohit Srivastava

A brinjal-coloured Honda scooter stands in front of my house today.

But a long time ago ...

... I was working in
a post office just
outside the city.

At work I daydreamed
of places — mountains,
oceans, forests — I longed
to explore the world!

OUT

So, one day I purchased a bicycle.

From then on, I would ride far away into the wind's embrace.

I rode to familiar towns. I rode to unfamiliar towns. I rode to places where there were no people at all ...

I wished I could keep on riding forever.

So I applied for long leave.

I planned a trip from Mangalore via Hassan. It was a long way to travel but I believed that I could do it!

I rode for two days, in rain and in shine, elated at my new freedom.

The journey was a beautiful one. I crossed lush green forests and soft rolling hills.

The rainy season had just arrived, but getting wet in the drizzle was a joy.

120 KM

HASSAN

On my third day, I was riding down a steep rocky hill when ...

POP
hssss!

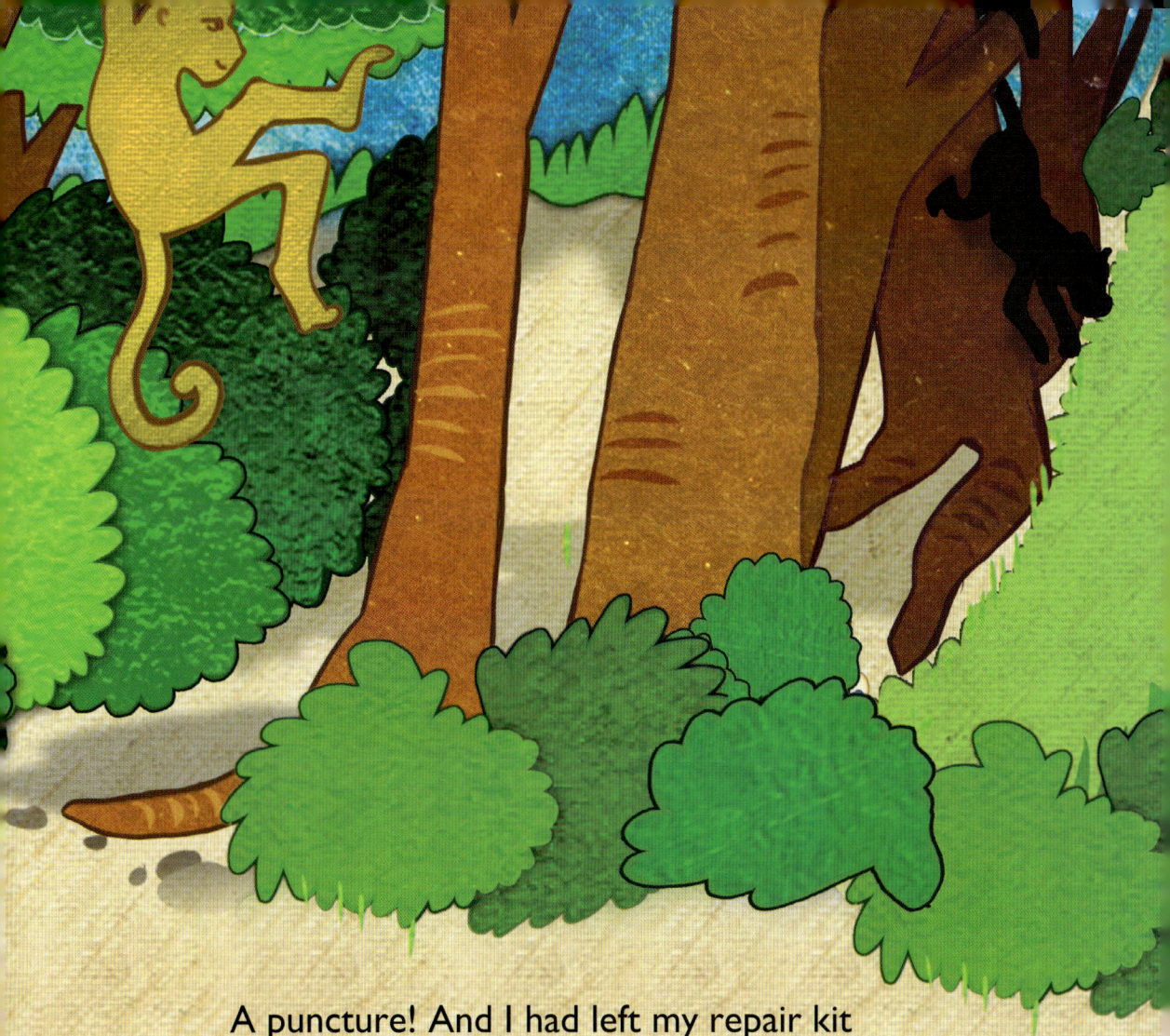

A puncture! And I had left my repair kit
and air pump at home!

I started walking, pushing my bicycle.
There were trees all around with large
swaying jackfruits and leaping monkeys.

There was no one around. I felt
like I was on a secret path of some
mysterious world.

Suddenly, it started to rain. Hard.

Pearls of rain dropped on my head and shoulders and the cold began to spread through my body.

I had no idea how far I had walked.

Over the fury of the rain, I heard a voice yelling to me.

A small boy stood at the doorway of a little hut, beckoning me to come in.

He asked, "Where are you from?"

"Mangalore," I said.

"All that way by bicycle? It's 200 kilometres from here!" said the boy. He stared at me in wonder. "Can you really travel that far by bicycle?"

I nodded.

"To the Himalayas?"

"Mm."

"To Pakistan?"

"If you set your heart on it, you can go anywhere."

The boy began to frown.

"I badly want a bicycle but Amma won't buy me one."

I took one look at his mother. I understood why.

"You're still a small boy. When you grow up, Amma will definitely buy you one."

"But who'll teach me to ride?"

"I will," I said, "as soon as the rain stops."

He began to pretend he was riding a bicycle around the room.

He held on to the imaginary handlebars, making a whooshing sound. He swerved to avoid an imaginary bus.

"Brake, brake!" I yelled.

We both burst out laughing. Like brothers, we shared the same streak of madness.

That night, he went on and on
about Bangalore, Lalbagh, Cubbon
Park and Ulsoor Lake.

"I'll visit them all someday,
on a bicycle, just like you!" he said.

His eyes shone.

The next morning the rain stopped. The boy and I went to a bicycle shop in the next town to fix the puncture.

On the way back, I said
to the boy, "Hop on!"

His joy knew no bounds.

I held the bicycle steady as he straightened his back and reached for the pedals.

He was small for the bicycle but not by too much. He started to roll forwards.

"I feel like I am flying!" he exclaimed.

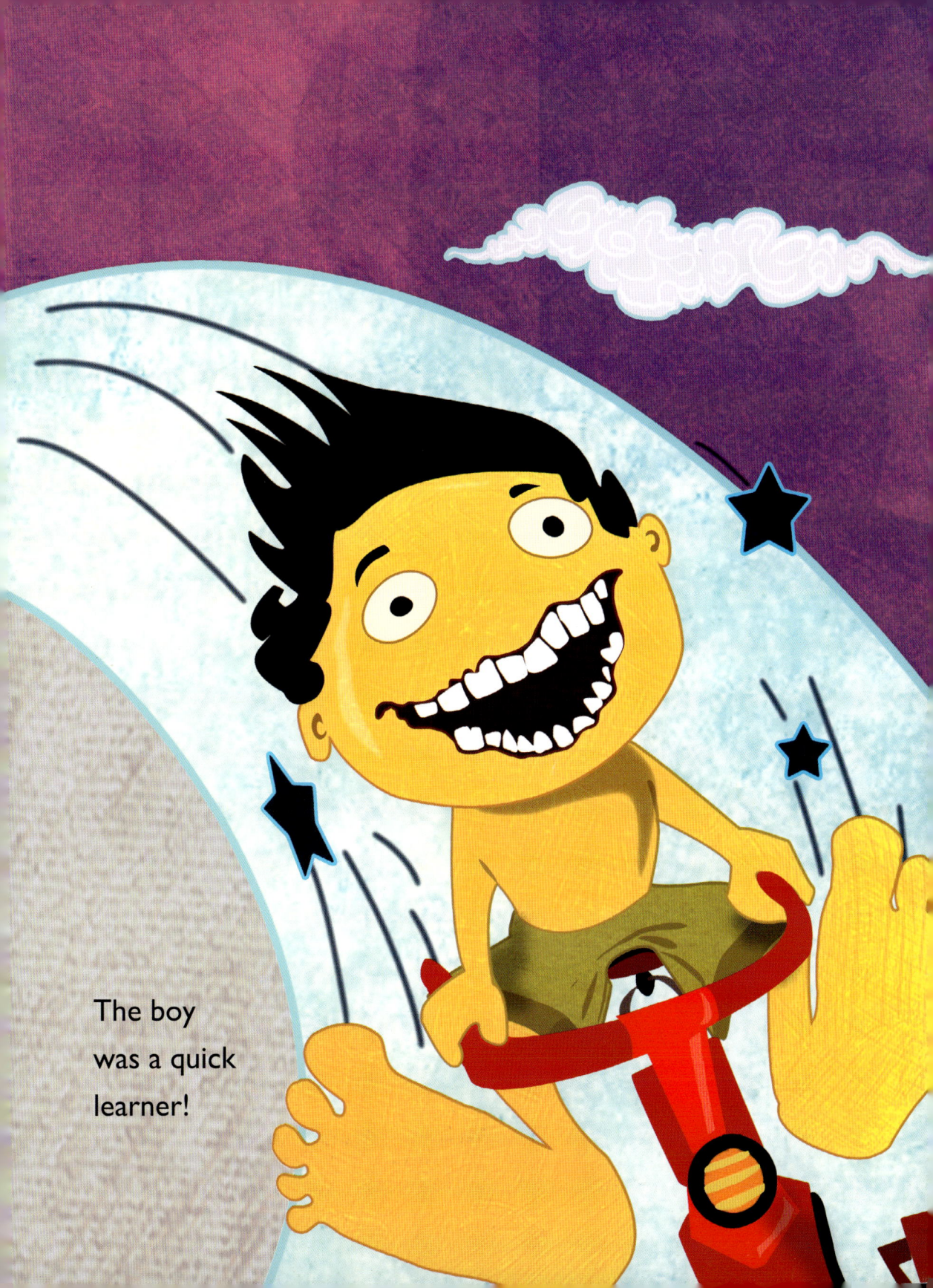

The boy
was a quick
learner!

The next morning, it was
time for me to leave. The boy
waited in front of the house
as I gathered my things.

He stood next to the bicycle, as if he was about to ride away on it.

He walked me to the
boundary of his town.

And then he said,
"Would you mind if I
rode around the block
one last time? I will come
right back!"

"Okay. But ..." Before I
could finish, he was away!

I watched cycle rickshaws,
auto rickshaws with their
yellow tops, lorries, and
many people moving in
every direction.

As he disappeared
round the corner,
I thought of his
family, his dreams,
his passion.

At that moment, a bus to Hassan
stopped in front of me.

Hassan, Bangalore

I came to a sudden
decision ...

I quickly climbed on, smiling.
The bus left immediately.

I looked down the street and
thought I could see his face,
beaming at me from afar.

Paavannan, a prolific writer, translator and editor, began writing in the 80s. Six collections of his stories, two novellas and a poetry collection have been published. His novel *Sidharalgal* recieved an award from the Government of Tamil Nadu in 1990. *Paaymara Kappal* was selected as the best novel for 1995 by Ilakkiya Chintanai and Thirupur Thamizh Changam. He won the Katha Award for Creative Fiction in 1998 for his Tamil story "Payanam." He has edited an anthology of Kannada Dalit writings and a collection of modern Kannada poems. He is by nature a wanderer and fond of travelling. This story is about a small boy he came across on one such occasion.

N Kalyan Raman, a technocrat, has written book reviews, articles and essays in English and Tamil. He translated Bertolt Brecht's *The Exception and The Rule* into Tamil in 1978.

Ayush Rajvanshi is a graduate from the National Institute of Design in Animation and Film Design. He has designed shows for Sesame Street in India and worked on projects like the Terra Quiz and Wills India Fashion Week. His short film "The Earth Story" was selected to open the UNESCO conference on climate change in Copenhagen.

Mohit Srivastava is a Bombay based award winning artist and storyteller.

KATHA

Copyright © Katha, 2014
Adapted from "The Journey"
published in *Katha Prize Stories Vol 7*
Illustrations copyright © Ayush Rajvanshi & Mohit Srivastava, 2014
All rights reserved. No part of this book may be reproduced or utilized in any form without the prior written permission of the publisher.
Printed at RaveIndia, New Delhi
ISBN 978-93-82454-20-5

KATHA is a registered nonprofit organization devoted to enhancing the joys of reading amongst children and adults. Katha Schools are situated in the slums and streets of Delhi and tribal villages of Arunachal Pradesh.
A3 Sarvodaya Enclave, Sri Aurobindo Marg
New Delhi 110 017
Phone: 4141 6600 . 4182 9998 . 2652 1752
Fax: 2651 4373
E-mail: marketing@katha.org, Website: www.katha.org

Ten per cent of sales proceeds from this book will support the quality education of children studying in Katha Schools.
Katha regularly plants trees to replace the wood used in the making of its books.

First Reprint 2015, Second Reprint 2017